Sunshine Warrior

Story and Pictures by

Jennifer Okubo

AuthorHouse™
1663 Liberty Drive
Bloomington, IN 47403
www.authorhouse.com
Phone: 1 (833) 262-8899

Because of the dynamic nature of the Internet, any web addresses or links contained in this book may have changed since publication and may no longer be valid. The views expressed in this work are solely those of the author and do not necessarily reflect the views of the publisher, and the publisher hereby disclaims any responsibility for them.

Any people depicted in stock imagery provided by Getty Images are models, and such images are being used for illustrative purposes only.
Certain stock imagery © Getty Images.

This book is printed on acid-free paper.

ISBN: 978-1-6655-0104-0 (sc)
ISBN: 978-1-6655-0103-3 (e)

Library of Congress Control Number: 2020918584

Print information available on the last page.

Published by AuthorHouse 10/06/2020

authorHOUSE®

Dedication. . .To my little sunshine

☺ Smiling is a beautiful thing, a symbol of peace & love. Smile from your heart and everyone will feel your happiness. Always share your smile with the world, it's a gift, an act of kindness, it is love. ☺

There was a time in the world when there was great sadness. The darkness had infected millions of people. Masks were worn to help from spreading the sadness to others. The world had basically stopped. People didn't know how to handle such sorrow.

Then came a little girl, named Lennox. She didn't understand why people chose to be so sad. There are so many things in this world to be grateful for. Lennox loved to laugh, dance and sing no matter what the day had to bring.

She would draw pictures for her friends and family. Her parents told her that she had a special gift of making people smile. She was their little sunshine.

Lennox would look out her window and watch people walk past her home. They all looked so sad, even the dogs. Lennox had such a big heart and wanted to spread some of her love.

One day, a thought popped into her mind. She went and told her parents. They thought it was brilliant. They helped her gather up all the supplies she needed and off she went.

She pulled her wagon out to the front fence and she started painting her favorite flower, a sunflower. A woman stopped and asked, "Why are you painting on your fence?" Lennox turned around with a big smile and said, "I'm doing it for you, to make you smile."

The woman first looked confused. Then there was a moment that Lennox felt it in her heart that the woman was smiling behind her mask. She cleaned up and ran inside to tell her parents about her day. She told them, she gave a woman a little bit of her sunshine.

She was out there every day, painting away. Lennox would always put her paint brush down when people stopped by to say hello. She enjoyed their compliments. She even took requests on what to paint next.

She painted a whole garden on her fence. She even included the garden creatures, from frogs to fairies. She painted from her heart. Their home even started to glow. It was looking so bright that she decided to paint a rainbow too!

19

Lennox was so busy painting her fence that she didn't notice that the whole neighborhood was glowing too!! She felt it in her heart that things were changing. The entire neighborhood was getting brighter by the day.

It was fun for Lennox to see all the wonderful changes. The changes weren't just in her neighborhood. It was spreading throughout the world. The air was cleaner. The waters were clearer. The wildlife were dancing & singing louder.

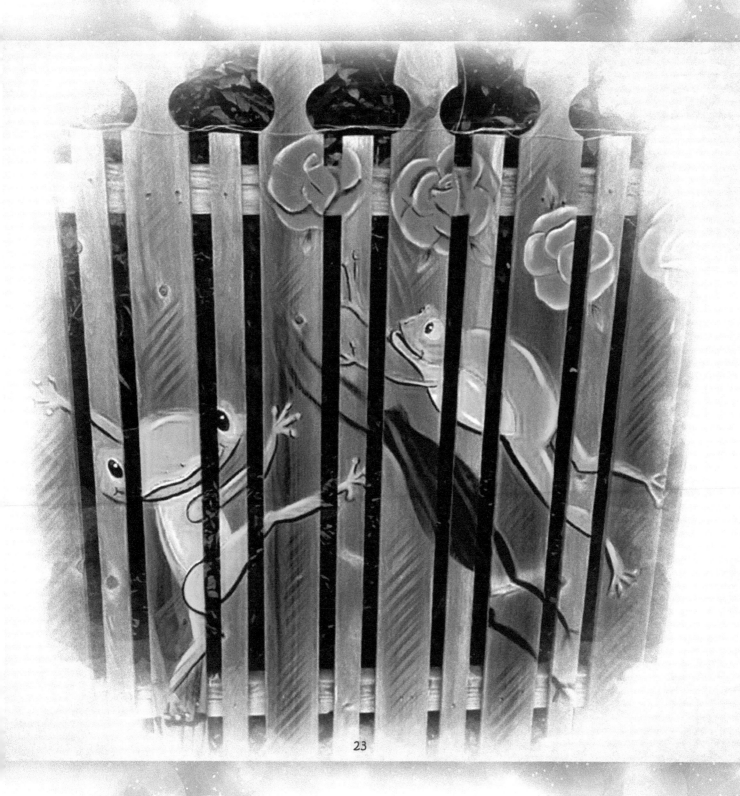

23

The neighbors had planted beautiful lush gardens all around their homes. People were laughing and smiling. Masks were no longer needed. There was no more sadness!

25

Lennox's parents were so proud of their little sunshine. They always taught her to be kind to all people, animals, and the environment. Kindness and willingness to help others goes a long way.

27

A gesture like a smile, is so simple but so powerful. Lennox knew that helping the people smile would be a great way to spread joy & love.

Lennox's heart was so full! She is now known throughout the world as the Sunshine Warrior...one smile at a time.